World's Weirdest Bugs

World's Weirdest BUGS

THE TINY ALIENS AMONG US

Paul Zborowski

young reed

First published in 2018 by Reed New Holland Publishers Pty Ltd
London • Sydney • Auckland

131–151 Great Titchfield Street, London WIW 5BB, UK
1/66 Gibbes Street, Chatswood, NSW 2067, Australia
5/39 Woodside Avenue, Northcote, Auckland 0627, New Zealand

newhollandpublishers.com

ISBN 978 1 92158 036 9

Group Managing Director: Fiona Schultz
Publisher: Simon Papps
Editor: Bill Twyman
Designer: Andrew Davies
Production Director: James Mills-Hicks
Printer: Times International Printers, Malaysia

10 9 8 7 6 5 4 3 2 1

Keep up with New Holland Publishers on Facebook
www.facebook.com/NewHollandPublishers

CONTENTS

How Weird Can It Get? 6

Fungus Zombies 8

Alien Grasshoppers 10

Giraffe Weevils 12

Frass and Fluff 14

What Else Comes Out of Your Bum? Explosive insects 16

Follow the Leader – Processionary Caterpillars 18

Membracids – The Treehoppers 20

Eight-legged Freaks 22

I am a Rock 24

Who Nose Best? The Lantern Flies 26

The Eyes Have it 28

Antler Flies 30

You Are What You Eat 32

The Hoppers Not In Your Garden 34

Tortoise Beetles 36

Don't Eat This 38

How Hairy Can You Get? 40

Life Without Rain – Namib Desert Beetles 42

Other Worthy Mentions 44

Do You Want to Know More? 46

Picture Credits 46

Index 48

And when all is said and done, 'weird' is a matter of taste, and perspective. If you imagine yourself their size, the amount of detail in insect structures that becomes apparent is staggering. This fairly common caterpillar, when looking straight at us, is more than a bit odd.

INTRODUCTION: HOW WEIRD CAN IT GET?

Over a million species of insects are already named, catalogued and pictured. Theories as to how many are still to be named in collections, and discovered for the first time in the wild, vary considerably. However, a figure of over two million is conservative.

Imagine natural selection – the environmental forces acting on the survival of a species in a particular habitat, working over millions of years to adapt forms and behaviour for survival. As these changes are driven by random mutations in huge populations of a species, some of these mutations are neutral. They neither hinder nor help the species to survive.

However, to us observers some of these mutations can be pretty weird. The palette available is almost infinite, the shapes also. Why not have wild eyes, or bizarre lumps, spines and dooverlackies? Whatever doesn't hurt survival can stay and develop further over time.

And then there are the changes that developed because they did aid survival. The perfect camouflage, or prey hunting aid, extreme habitat adaptation, or super sense – these can get pretty weird too.

Here are example stories from all over the world. The subject is endless, so the last few chapters simply touch on more weird stories for the reader to investigate further – the so-called 'honorary mentions' in this hall of weird fame. And no apologies for squeezing in one non-insect chapter. The spider relatives, the Opiliones on page 22, are just too quirky to ignore.

FUNGUS ZOMBIES

Walking in very damp tropical jungles, you sometimes come across these weird sights. Is it an ant?

Actually, it is an ex-ant, murdered by a tropical fungus. The fungus' tiny spores can slide between the plates of an insect's exoskeleton. It then feeds on the living innards until it is ready to form a mushroom to release spores. To spread spores as far as possible it needs to be high up, so it literally forces the 'zombie' victim to crawl up onto a thin branch. The fungus then kills the insect and sprouts through its body. This releases spores to rain down onto more insects.

This exceedingly fluffy cicada is not wearing a fur coat, but is covered by the spongy fungus which just killed it after devouring its innards.

This gothic looking moth from New Guinea is not really a whole new family of spined insects. The spines are the mushrooms of the fungus which killed it.

This killer fungus in Australia subdued the otherwise scary stinging paper wasp. Instead of mushrooms, it releases its spores from many fine strands.

This duo of plant hoppers almost look like a heavy fall of snow caught them out – in the middle of a hot tropical forest. The killer fungus which took their lives acted so fast it managed to coordinate their position for the best dispersal of its spores.

ALIEN GRASSHOPPERS

With over 25,000 species of grasshoppers and crickets, the common green hopper in your yard is not the only shape to have evolved. The weirder end of this group resides in South America. These long, skinny species look like aliens from a sci-fi story. They are slow – some mimic sticks – and they seem to stare back at you with attitude.

The four species shown here are all from the Amazonian forests of Ecuador. The line that looks like a mouth is just one of many facial segments. Like all insects, their real jaws move from side to side – in this case to eat leaves.

This pinhead model of a grasshopper from New Guinea is unrelated to the weird ones above. However its tiny head is worthy of mention. It's all eyes! Where is the brain?

GIRAFFE WEEVILS

'Giraffe' weevils is a very apt name for a number of species in Madagascar. They have a wild body shape, with a very mechanical-looking hinge between the extra long neck and head – the males' necks are easily longer than their bodies.

These insects belong to the Family Attelabidae, which roll leaves to create a home for their eggs and larvae.

The red species below is famous, but there are other species in the forests and savannahs of Madagascar

If the general appearance is not weird enough, when the weevils mate, the exaggerated body shape become even more bizarre, making it hard to see where one begins and the other ends.

FRASS AND FLUFF

Primitive sap-sucking bugs, called hoppers, often look very different in their young nymph stages compared to their adult shape. These frass-producing creatures feed by sucking the sweet sap from plants. They suck a lot more than is needed for food, and exude the extra sugary, waxy residue to cover their bodies completely, or form a filamentous tail – like a more solid form of fairy floss. This strategy helps to hide their little soft bodies and gives them protection from ants, which come to lick the sugar.

These nymphs make waxy secretions from their tail end only and grow them out continuously. The end breaks off and is replaced. Top image is from New Caledonia, the right one is from Madagascar, and on the left is a striped Flatid nymph from Australia.

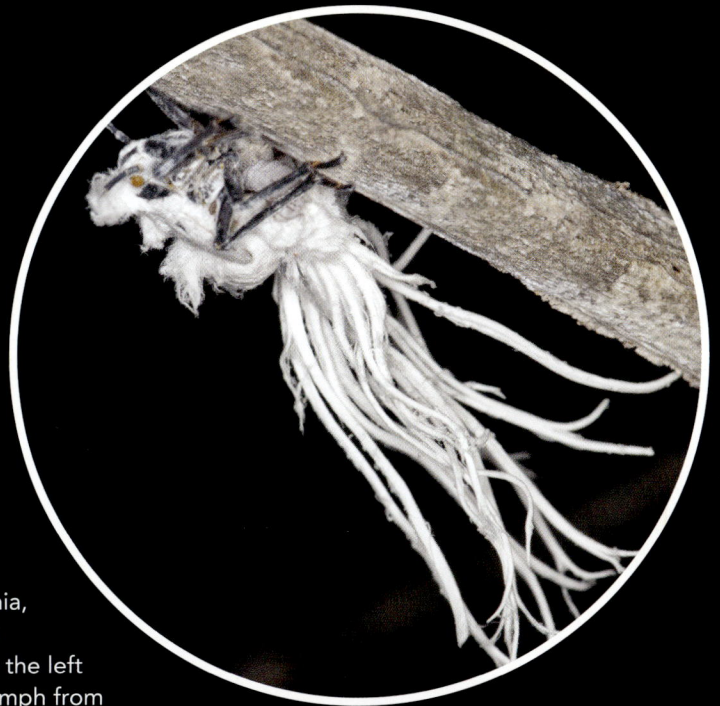

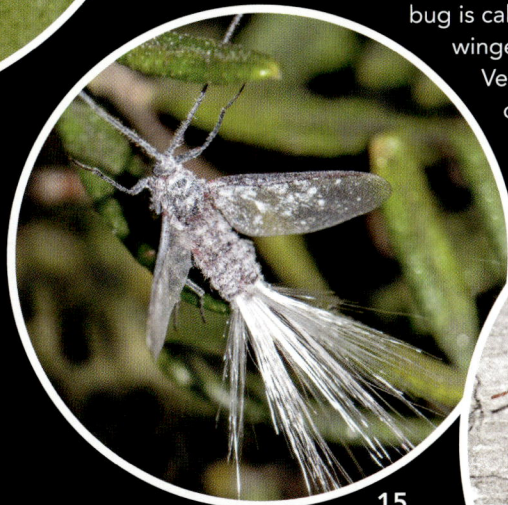

Only some of these insects carry on the frass habit in their adult stage. This oddly named sap-sucking bug is called a paradise fly. At least the tailed, winged male, flying in the sun, fits the name. Very few people get to see the seriously odd, secretive, wingless female, below.

WHAT ELSE COMES OUT OF YOUR BUM? EXPLOSIVE INSECTS

EXPLODING ANTS

All ants will fight to the death to defend their nests and most species have a fighting chance of surviving. However, several species of ants in Malaysia and Borneo have evolved a dubious method of attack and defence.

Exploding ants mount suicide attacks guaranteed to kill their enemy. They use their strong jaws to grip the enemy ant's antenna or leg then rupture their own bodies, covering their enemy in a thick yellow goo which sticks like glue. The enemy ant does not die straight away, but it cannot feed, sense or even see, and will die very soon.

The little ant taking on the monster ant above is the original exploding ant. Note the mess on the monster's head, which it cannot clean off – this goo will kill it. Much has been written about the exploding ant's habits and internal body bits, as well as the arguments for and against a suicide attack strategy. The little ants on the right are from another Malaysian family. Recently, they have been found to be using similar tactics. In their case, the yellow structures on their backs do the exploding, covering their enemies in a similar gooey glue.

BOMBARDIER BEETLES

Sometimes truth is stranger than fiction. The bombardier beetles are a group of ground hunting beetles in the family Carabidae, found on most continents. The picture above right is typical of the species, and the picture above left is the same beetle defending itself.

It holds two chemicals in separate large glands near its bum, which explode instantly when mixed. This produces a squirt of boiling hot, acrid, smoky liquid. The beetle can control the direction of the squirt, and can do so repeatedly. Each explosion can be heard as a loud hiss – enough shock, horror and pain to scare off most intruders, including giant predators like mammals and birds.

Like other ground beetles they spend most of their lives hunting for insects, worms and snails. On the right are two stamps which commemorate this famous weirdo.

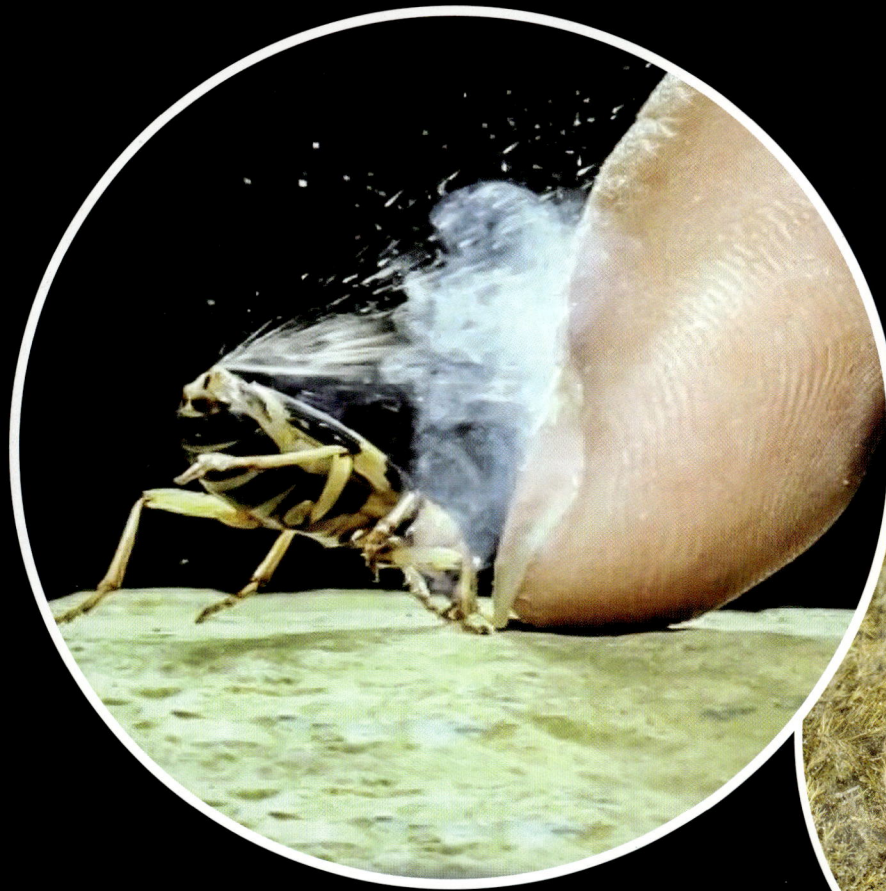

Bombardier beetle

FOLLOW THE LEADER –
PROCESSIONARY CATERPILLARS

This is the caterpillar of a large hairy moth in Australia. There is nothing remarkable about the adult, but these bristle-covered larvae are odd and dangerous. The bristles and hairs are not just annoying but toxic to all who touch them.

They feed on Acacia trees in large groups, spending the days in big bristly, hairy, impenetrable silk bags, and all night devouring every last leaf. When they need to move to another tree, they do so in a procession, touching nose to bum to avoid getting separated (below).

However, if the leader is stopped or killed, they will bunch up and often find themselves in a circle. If this happens, the circle of caterpillars will turn on the spot until they die.

A bunch or horde of the caterpillars preparing a daytime defensive bag shelter. Extra, loose, venomous bristles and hairs are caught in the silk structure. And two happy caterpillars meeting in the middle as they devour another leaf.

MEMBRACIDS – THE TREEHOPPERS

There are over 3,000 species of these playful over-adorned sap-sucking bugs in the family Membracidae. Treehoppers are mainly found in the tropics – most species live in Central and South America.

Most treehoppers have at least a hump on their backs, but in some species this has evolved into more and more elaborate structures – strange horns, spheres, spines and wiggly things. Their young are called nymphs and often look completely different to the adults.

They come in just about every shade of the rainbow – a feast for the eyes of the explorer.

Two of the more famous membracids, from Ecuador, with structures that are just plain weird. (above, and below right)

Treehoppers are also good parents, defending their young by living in colonies. Here, Acacia spine-mimicking hoppers keep their babies safe between them on a branch.

This treehopper family from Belize highlights the difference between adults and nymphs. The spines on the red babies are lost as they mature. The other examples below are from Australia, the next two are from New Guinea, and the last is from Costa Rica.

EIGHT-LEGGED FREAKS

Take a peek at some non-insect critters that deserve the title of weird. Spiders are not the only eight-legged creatures. The Opiliones Class, sometimes known as harvestmen, live in forests, especially in the tropics.

They have super long legs and all their main body parts are fused into one almost spherical shape. They look like the Martian machine walkers in H.G. Wells' invasion book. Their eyes are on a raised pedestal in the middle of their body.

They are harmless to us.

Apart from their kooky appearance, their behaviour can be a bit strange too. The three here, on a leaf in Ecuador, bob up and down like springs for much of the day. Go figure!

Another eight-legged group are the whip scorpions. They look so strange that the Harry Potter movie team used them as scary magical creatures without altering a whisker.

Stick spiders may not be the weirdest eight-legged creatures, but their attitude makes up for it. Note the casual way this 'I am just a little twig' spider sways in the breeze, hanging by one foot to one silk thread.

This variation on a centipede is oddly called a 'house' centipede. The super long spindly legs don't look strong enough to support it. However, it is a very swift runner and hunter. Some species are scary large – up to 15cm (6in) long.

I AM A ROCK

Not all deserts are made of sand. Small polished stones, known as gibbers, make up vast areas of the interior of Australia.

   Many species of grasshoppers have evolved the appearance of stones to live disguised among them. Other bugs in stony deserts in Asia, North America and Africa have similar adaptations too. Find the two critters in the main picture.

The beautiful red and white marble in this gibber desert is perfectly matched by a stone hopper.

This Australian grasshopper goes further than rock mimicry. It has lines of dust patterns separating several 'rocks' to further confuse any predators

WHO NOSE BEST – THE LANTERN FLIES

Lantern flies have no lights, and are not flies. This group of insects was named by someone who thought their outrageous noses were shaped like ancient lanterns. They belong to a sap-sucking bug family called Fulgoridae – not all of them have funny noses!

However, the ones which have this weird schnozz often combine it with imaginative patterns and decorations. The structure is not a real nose, and is actually largely empty inside. Apart from possibly being part of courtship display, its function is unknown.

Although the family was first discovered in South America, all the species on this spread are from Borneo, and quite large – between 4–7cm (1.5–3in) long.

THE EYES HAVE IT

As discussed in the beginning of the book, details like the shade or pattern of eyes rarely have an impact on the survival value of the insect. Given the vast numbers and fast breeding cycles of insects, weird mutations can enter and stay in a population.

Flies have taken this eye mutation further than other insects, and also have the most number of facets in their compound eyes. Up to 12,000 separate facets, each acting as a simple eye, can detect movement across a very wide angle with fantastic accuracy. That's why you cannot sneak up on a housefly.

The fly above is a hover or drone fly from Australia.

House fly, world

Fruit fly, Australia

Fruit fly, Costa Rica

March fly, Australia

Fruit fly, New Guinea

March fly, New Guinea

March fly, Costa Rica

Monkey grasshopper, Madagascar

March fly, Australia

29

ANTLER FLIES

On the previous pages, eye patterns were king. But why stop there? Why not put the eyes on the ends of antlers? Why not emulate large creatures with antlers, like deer, and use the eye antlers to fight?

Enter the antler flies. The males of these tropical species have spectacular eye stalks, and do ritual combat with other males to impress the less-antlered females. Imagine what their eyes see as they bash each other with them!

This African example is not so dainty – its antlers look like a hammerhead. The fights must be rugged!

The fly above, from Malaysia, has extreme eye antlers. Note the female on the right, which has much smaller eye stalks.

Not all antler fly males come with bigger antlers than the females. In some species the male and female have the same size eye structures. Here, in a very confusing profusion of spines, eyes and legs, is an evenly matched pair from Thailand.

Many insects and spiders mimic ants, because ants are a nasty prey to try to catch and eat. This antler fly seems to be mimicking ants too, except for the much too obvious, non-ant like eyes.

This very untidy mess is an assassin bug from Africa. A predator of ants, it covers its body in their dry bodies and other rubbish.

YOU ARE WHAT YOU EAT

There are many examples of camouflage and deception in the insect world. Among the rarer stories – the concept of becoming what you eat!

The katydid on the left ate red leaves and turned red. In adult life it will eat green leaves and be a proper green cricket.

Or there is the gory and fun adaptation of covering yourself with the bodies of the your victims and other general rubbish. Hard for bigger predators to see what is going on.

The creature above and right, is a nymph of a lacewing. Its body is a bit like a caterpillar, but here only its head, with huge piercing jaws, protrudes from under the mountain of dead bodies and rubbish. It has sucked out the contents of the dry husks. These insects are so voracious, the theory is that the reason their eggs are laid on stalks, above right, is so that the newly hatched babies don't eat each other straight away.

There are many insect species that have evolved to resemble bark, lichen and so on, to hide in their habitat. This Geometrid moth caterpillar, already weird enough in shape, looks exactly like the yellow lichen around it because it covers itself in it.

THE HOPPERS NOT IN YOUR GARDEN

There are many thousands of species of small sap-sucking bugs called plant hoppers. All make a living sucking the sugary fluids flowing through plants. Some, but not all, actually do hop.

During their immature stages they are often patterned and even shaped differently. Their spectacular patterns, employing a huge variety of deep and exuberant shades, serve as a warning to predators that they eat poisonous plants.

They are also one of the best examples of evolution at work – random and visually extreme mutations, which do no harm, proliferate in these species. These examples are from tropical rainforests all over the world – the green species on the top left of page 35 is more like what you would see in your garden.

TORTOISE BEETLES

Rarely are insect common names as apt as in the case of the tortoise beetles. These species of leaf beetles in the family Chrysomelidae have expanded wing cases and other parts on the top of their bodies which act like a shell.

More weirdly, in many of them the expanded parts are see-through, showing their large sucker-pad like feet. When threatened they can sit flat with all body bits under the shell, just like a real tortoise. They are found all over the warmer parts of the world.

To our eyes this is an unfortunate pattern for any living creature to be displaying – the bulls-eye target symbol! Luckily for the beetle, to its predators the yellow and black mean danger, keep away.

Not all tortoise beetles are see-through. Some, like this one from Madagascar, channel their weird into ornate body shields and spines.

DON'T EAT THIS

There are several groups of insects which feed on dung and other poo. Most predators on the planet see this is as a total no-no. What better way to escape being a victim than to imitate poo? The more perfectly and imaginatively, the better.

Spiders are the true masters, as they can cheat and use several different types of silk web to imitate bird poo perfectly. They can even make it seem that the poo is oozing off their body onto the leaf. This master, right, also never needs to move – it attracts flies to itself with a smell gland, smelling – no not like poo – like rotting meat.

As well as spiders other insect species imitate bird poo – they just don't have silk to paint with. On the left, from top to bottom, are: a moth 'splat' in Madagascar, a weevil in Costa Rica, and a moth in Malaysia.

This is a very common insect. We know the adult as the orchard butterfly, with variations found near citrus plants in most of the world. The caterpillar, when bigger, is not remarkable. But when it first hatches, it perfectly imitates a bird splat. And best of all, the shiny texture of a fresh one.

There is of course an exception to every rule. 'Don't eat this' only refers to us humans. Butterflies love and need the chemicals in fresh bird poo and mammal pee.

HOW HAIRY CAN YOU GET?

Hairy caterpillars are a common sight and often lead to tears.

Many hairy species have 'urticating' hairs, designed to fall off and attach to your clothes and skin. These are often laced with irritating chemicals. Others keep their hair on but inject painful chemicals as you brush them. Others still have structures more like sea anemone tentacles, laced with a very similar toxin that hurts for many days.

Beware! Allergic reactions add another level of danger to the unwary.

This moth caterpillar, left, is mildly hairy when in a mild mood. It produces these red/black spiny hairs when attacked. Touching them releases toxins that are likely to be memorable.

Above is a cup moth caterpillar. They have special sea anemone-like tufts which pack the same stinging pain as that of sea anemones. Nature often uses the same idea twice, known as convergent evolution.

This spiny, hairy and tentacled species lives in Ecuador. At least one of its defences is bound to cause pain.

40

Its not just caterpillars that excel in hairstyles. Adult moths also can be spectacularly hairy, though usually without added irritating chemicals. Both these moths are from Australia, and somehow manage to see where they are going and fly in spite of all that hair-air resistance.

LIFE WITHOUT RAIN – NAMIB DESERT BEETLES

The Namib Desert in south-west Africa is an ocean of sand waves, sculpted to perfection every day by the wind. It may not rain a single drop here for years, and at a glance the desert looks lifeless.

However, the darkling beetle family Tenebrionidae includes a large number of species adapted to this life. They drink fog, which rolls in from the cold Atlantic Ocean on many days of the year. Ingenious behaviours help them capture this source of life.

This fog-drinking beetle gets up before sunrise and arches its body bum up towards the rolling fog. Moisture condenses on its shiny body and drips down to its mouth.

This beautiful, flat beetle swims inside the dunes during the day. The task is made easier by the backward pointing yellow hairs which make it very slippery. The pattern on its back has been painted on the shields of the local tribesmen.

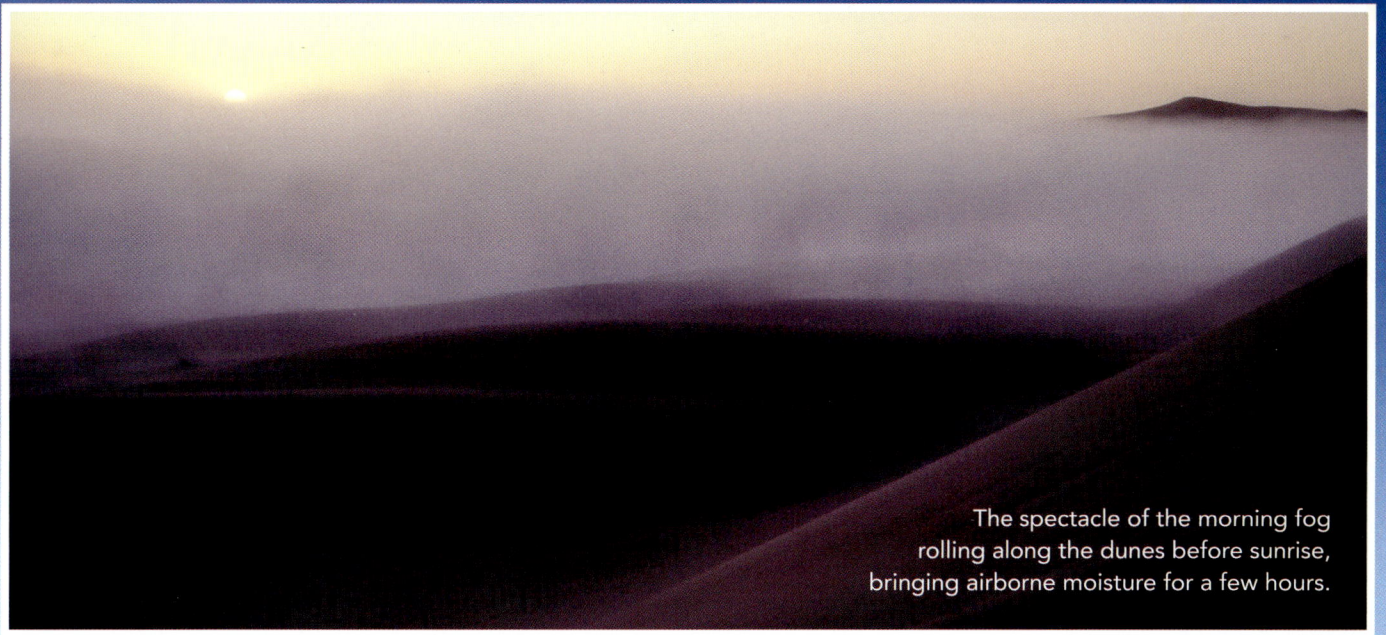

The spectacle of the morning fog rolling along the dunes before sunrise, bringing airborne moisture for a few hours.

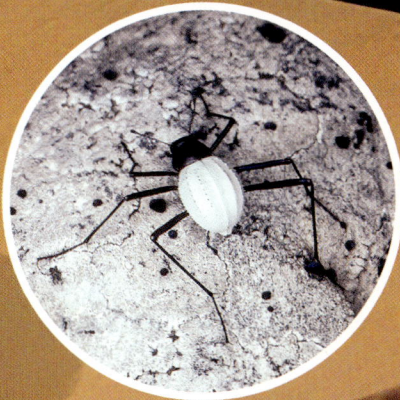

The Namib has one of the rarest sights in the insect world – a white beetle. This long-legged species runs fast and high off the sand. Its white back reflects some heat.

This flat darkling beetle digs furrows near the top of a dune facing the fog. Water condenses on the rough walls and the beetle drinks off the wet sand. During the day it escapes the fierce heat by swimming into the dune.

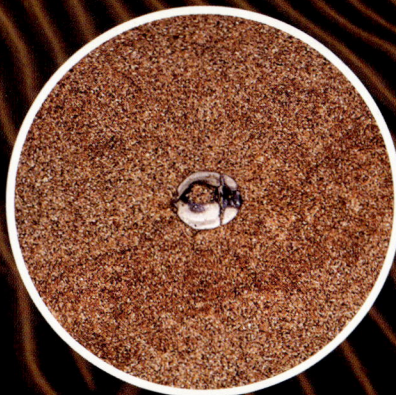

OTHER WORTHY MENTIONS

Where to from here? The insect world is endlessly surprising – too many stories for any one book. Go out and explore your local world and be surprised. Enjoy!

These small flies, called fungus gnats, spend their time hanging on spider webs. They even wobble the web for hours, and for some unknown reason, are neither caught in the glue, nor eaten by the spider.

Most termites, and all worker termites, have sideways-acting jaws for chewing through wood. However, one group of termites has soldiers with this squirt-gun head. They cover invading ants with a glue-like gunge.

This shiny domed 'beetle' is actually a fly. The so-called beetle flies are weird creatures with wings hidden under a beetle-like shell. This 0.4cm (⅛in) species is from Borneo.

In Central America, the land of the gold-loving Incas and Mayans, there lives a scarab beetle that looks like it's painted with gold. You wonder what these ancient people thought as it came to the light of their torches.

The family of tiger moths contains many species which eat poisonous plants and caterpillars, and store the toxins in their adult bodies. Their patterns warn other creatures that they are dangerous. However, this species does not want to be eaten to prove it is poisonous. It squirts out its poison in these interesting buckyball-like spheres.

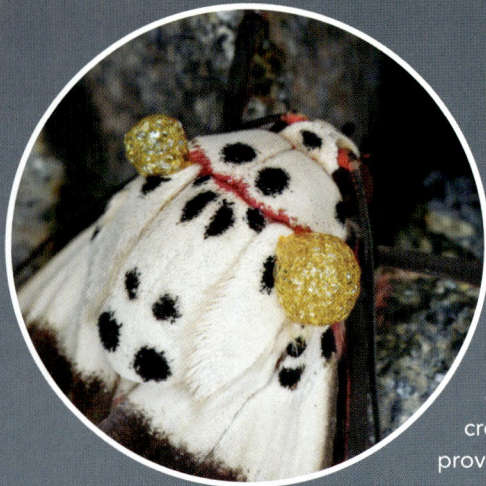

You may know the whirligig beetle, rushing around on the surface of ponds. It searches for insects that fall on the surface. But did you know it has two separate pairs of eyes, one for looking up out of the water, and one for looking down into the water?

Yes, the pet this boy is holding proudly, is a cockroach – one of the world's largest species. It lives in dry areas of Australia's north-east tropics, and is semi-social. The mothers feed their young in deep tunnels, and they hiss nicely.

Quite a scary encounter with a snake, until you know that this is a harmless, orchard butterfly caterpillar, only 5cm (2in) long. It relies on a scare tactic produced by suddenly exposing the false 'eyes'.

The larvae of flies known as torrent midges cling to rocks on waterfalls and rapids in fast-flowing mountain streams. They scrape algae and detritus off the rocks for food. Their secret is the six, octopus-like sucker pads on their bellies.

DO YOU WANT TO KNOW MORE?

BOOKS

An introduction to more weirdos, and a few reference works where you can learn more about insects in general.

Jones, Richard 2010. *Extreme Insects*, Harper Collins

Find a preview on this website:

www.theguardian.com/environment/gallery/2010/sep/24/
    extreme-insects-richard-jones

Mertz, Leslie 2007. *Extreme Insects (The Extreme Wonders Series)*, Harper Paperback

The Natural History Museum, London, 1995. *Megabugs, The Natural History Museum Book of Insects*, Carlton Books

Nichols, Catherine 2007. *The Most Extreme Bugs*, Animal Planet and Discovery Channel, Jossey-Bass publishers.

Worek, Michael 2013. *Weird Insects*, Firefly Books

Zborowski, Paul 2007. *Spiders, Snails and other Minibeasts of Australia*, Young Reed

Zborowski, Paul 2016. *Bloodsuckers*, Young Reed

Zborowski, Paul 2010. *Can You Find Me, Nature's Hidden Creatures*, Young Reed

Zborowski, Paul and Storey, Ross 2017. *A Field Guide to Insects in Australia*, Fourth Edition. Reed New Holland

THE WEB

Most museums around the world have great insect sites. Look for them locally, and visit the museums if you can.

Australian Museum insect pages
    australianmuseum.net.au/insects

Natural History Museum in London, insect site
    www.nhm.ac.uk/our-science/departments-and-staff/life-sciences/insects.html

General insect resources sites:

www.insects.org

www.insectimages.org

PICTURE CREDITS

page 6   Caterpillar by Jean and Fred Hort

page 15   Paradise flies by Jean and Fred Hort

page 15   Paradise bug by Jean and Fred Hort

page 17   Bombardier beetle exploding courtesy of Swedish Biomimetics 3000 AB www.swedishbiomimetics3000.com

page 17   Bombardier beetle by Owen Kelly

Moth caterpillar from Borneo

INDEX

Acacia 19

Adaptation 7

Africa 30, 32, 42, 43

Antler flies 4, 30, 31

Ants 8, 16

Aposematic 34, 35

Assassin bug 32

Attelabidae 12, 13

Australia 9, 15, 18, 19, 21, 24, 25, 29, 33, 33

Bat fly

Beetle flies 44

Belize 21

Bird poo 38, 39

Bird poo moth 38

Bird poo spider 39

Bird poo weevil 38

Bombardier beetle 17

Borneo 16, 26, 27

Butterfly 39

Camouflage 24, 25

Caterpillars 2, 18, 19, 40, 41, 45, 47

Centipede 23

Chinese Junk 45

Chrysomelidae 36, 37

Cicada 9

Cockroach 45

Costa Rica 21, 29, 38

Crickets 11

Crypsis 24, 25

Cup moth 40

Darkling beetles 42, 43

Desert 24, 2542, 43

Drone fly 28

Ecuador 10, 11, 40

Exploding ants 16

Evolution 7, 34, 35

Eyes 28, 29

Flatid 14, 15

Fluff 14, 15

Fungus gnats 44

Frass 14, 15

Fruit flies 29

Fulgoridae 26, 27

Fungus 8, 9

Fungus gnats 44

Geometrid moth 33

Giant cockroach 45

Gibber 24

Giraffe weevils 12, 13

Grasshoppers 1, 10, 11, 24, 25, 29

Habitat 7, 42, 43

Harvestman 22, 23

Hoppers 14, 15

House flies 29

Katydid 32

Killer fungus 8, 9

Lacewings 33

Lantern flies 26, 27

Madagascar 12, 13, 15, 29, 37, 38

Malaysia 16, 31, 38

March flies 29

Membracidae 20, 21

Mimicry 38, 39

Moths 18, 19, 38

Mutation 7

Namib Desert 42, 43

Namibia 42, 43

Natural selection 7

New Caledonia 15

New Guinea 9, 11, 21, 29

Nymph 14, 15, 33

Opiliones 22, 23

Orchard butterfly 38, 45

Owl butterfly 2

Paradise fly 15

Plant hoppers 9, 15

Poo 38, 39

Processionary caterpillars 18, 19

Sap-sucking bugs 34, 35

Scarab beetle 44

Silk 19

South America 10, 11, 40

Spiders 23

Tenebrionidae 42, 43

Termites 44

Thailand 31

Tiger moths 44

Torrent midge 45

Tortoise beetles 36, 37

Treehopper 20, 21

Urticating hairs 40, 41

Warning colors 1, 36

Wasp 9

Waterfall fly 44

Wax 14, 15

Weevil 12, 13, 38

Whip scorpion 23

Whirligig beetle 45

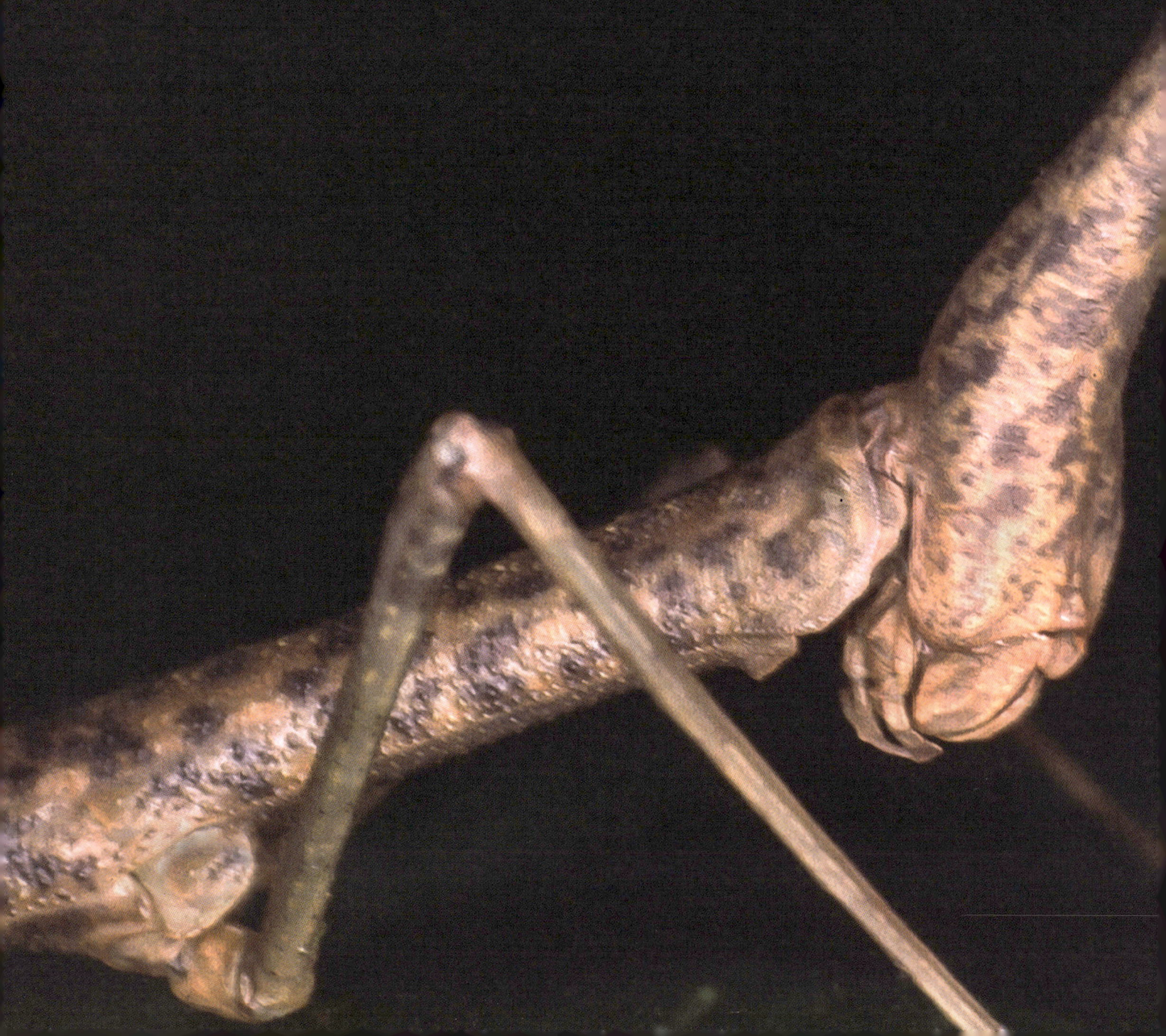